Malala Yousafzai

www.pegasusforkids.com

© **B. Jain Publishers (P) Ltd.** All rights reserved. No part of this book may be reproduced, stored in a retrieval system or transmitted, in any form or by any means, mechanical, photocopying, recording or otherwise, without any prior written permission of the publisher.

Published by Kuldeep Jain for B. Jain Publishers (P) Ltd., D-157, Sector 63, Noida - 201307, U.P
Registered office: 1921/10, Chuna Mandi, Paharganj, New Delhi-110055

Printed in India

Contents

5   Who is Malala Yousafzai?

6   Malala's Family

13   Early Life of Malala

24   Attempt of Assassination

40   Malala's Protest Continues

44   Malala's Speech at the United Nations

57   Knowing Malala

63   Awards and Accolades

65   Timeline

67   Activities

69   Glossary

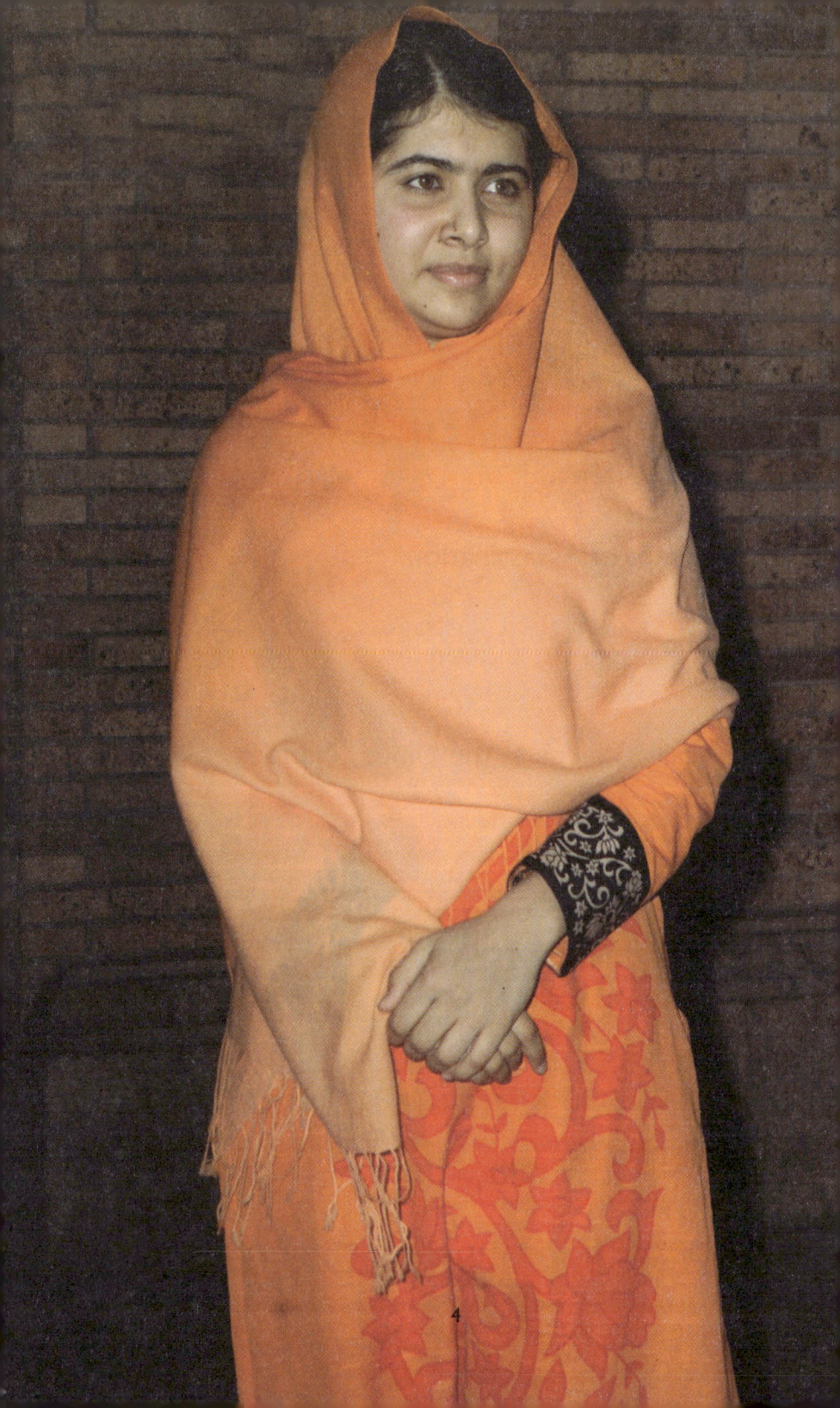

Who is Malala Yousafzai?

Malala Yousafzai is a Pakistani activist and spokesperson for women's right to education. She was shot in the head at a close range by a Taliban gunman in retaliation for her high-profile campaign for education of the girl child and criticism of the Taliban.

Although it was an inhuman and deadly attack by the Taliban, she survived the gunshot wound and has become a leading spokesperson for human rights, education and women's rights. Malala has been honoured with numerous peace awards, and is recipient of the Nobel Peace Prize in 2014. She received the award with Kailash Satyarthi, an Indian children's rights activist.

Malala's Family

Malala today has become a symbol of courage and conviction. She hails from an extremely enlightened family where her parents hold rather liberal viewpoints.

Malala once stated in an interview what it was like growing up in the Yousafzai home in their native Pakistan. She said, "We all were in a very small house, not rich economically, but rich in our values, in our ethics."

Malala's father, Ziauddin Yousafzai, is a prime example of rich ethics. A schoolteacher by profession, he started his own school in 1994 where he taught 1,100 students, including hundreds of girls. According to him, Pakistan has not improved in the last 20 years in terms of gender equality. Ziauddin's efforts to educate both genders gave Malala the idea to start the 'Malala Fund', which offers scholarships to girls undergoing unlawful child labour.

Given the background of relationship and gender statuses in Pakistan, it is remarkable how Malala's parents defied their traditional culture, which revolved around dominating the girl child.

Ziauddin once said while talking about the violation of women's rights, "Fathers are usually known by their sons. But I'm one of the few fathers who is known by his daughter, and I'm proud of it."

During the same conversation, he referred to women's plight throughout patriarchal history as the "study of a woman is the study of injustice, inequality, violence and exploitation".

Malala has two younger brothers—Khushal, aged 14, and Atal, aged 9. While it was a norm for people in their country to have at least 7 or 8 children in the family, the Yousafzai couple restricted their family to a total number of just 3.

Ziauddin explains how Middle Eastern history sees an ideal daughter as one who is quiet and submissive. In a sense of creating gender equality within the Yousafzai family, Malala acknowledged that her mother, Torpekai, does not get a lot of recognition for her supporting role.

Speaking about the Malala Fund in an interview, Malala said, "My mother always encourages us to continue this

campaign. She believes that what we are doing is the truth and we should never be afraid of telling the truth."

Torpekai recently proved her support for her daughter's humanitarian efforts by disregarding decades of deprived educational opportunities when she learned to read! This is an achievement that only 47 percent of Pakistani women on average realize.

Although her comments in an NBC News story were addressed to her father, Malala's words reflect her inspiring feelings and respect for both her parents, "I'm thankful to my father for not clipping my wings, for letting me fly and achieve my goals, for showing the world that a girl is not supposed to be a slave. A girl has the power to go forward in her life."

The ongoing story of the Yousafzais is one of a family fighting for peace and equality in a harsh world around them. It is one that we should all learn to emulate.

Early Life of Malala

Malala is a Pakistani activist who spoke out publicly against the Taliban's prohibition on the education of girls. She was born on July 12, 1997 in Mingora, the Swat District of north-west Pakistan to a Sunni Muslim family. She was named Malala, which means 'grief stricken', after a famous female Pashtun poet and warrior from Afghanistan.

She gained global attention when she survived an assassination attempt at age 15. In 2014, Malala and Kailash Satyarthi were jointly awarded the Nobel Prize for Peace, recognizing their efforts on behalf of children's rights.

Malala hails from a family of liberal views. Her father is an outspoken social activist, poet and educator, who used to run a chain of public schools in Swat. He is known for his advocacy of education for girl children. As a young girl, Malala excelled in her studies.

Her father established and administered the school she attended—Khushal Girls High School & College—in the city of Mingora. He would always encourage and support his daughter to follow in his path.

Swat Valley under Taliban Rule

In the year 2007, the Swat Valley, once a vacation destination, was invaded by the Taliban. Led by Maulana Fazlullah, the Pakistani Taliban began imposing strict Islamic law, destroying or shutting down girls' schools, banning women from any active role in society, and carrying out suicide bombings.

Shutting Off Girls' Schools

During this period, the Taliban's military hold on the area intensified. At times, Malala reported hearing artillery from the advancing Taliban forces. As the Taliban took control of the area, they issued edicts banning television, music, and banning women from going shopping and limiting women's education. Many girls' schools were blown up. As a consequence, students were forced to stay at home, due to the fear of Taliban attack.

Initially, Malala found the happenings around her too difficult to believe. She would often console herself saying it wouldn't last. How could the Taliban stop her and her friends from going to school? But her friends wondered who could stop the Taliban from doing it; after all, they had already got away with blowing up hundreds of schools.

Malala's Protest

On September 1, 2008, when Malala was just 11 years old, her father took her to a local press club in Peshawar to protest against the school closings, and she gave her first speech—"How Dare the Taliban Take Away My Basic Right to Education?"

Her speech was publicized throughout Pakistan. Towards the end of 2008, the Taliban announced that all girls' schools in Swat would be shut down on January 15, 2009.

Widespread protests caused the Taliban to change their minds and allow girls up to the age of 10 to attend school. Malala and her friends, who were too old to be allowed to go to school in their normal clothes, hid their school books under their shawls on their way to the school. The girls' head teacher called it 'the secret school'.

A few days later, the Pakistan army ordered the inhabitants of the Swat Valley to leave their homes. The reason cited was their plan to launch a ferocious attack on the Taliban. Over a million people turned into refugees overnight in their own country. Malala's family left the valley and were only able to return home three months later. Although the Pakistani army claimed to have defeated the Taliban, soon the Taliban started to blow up schools in the Swat Valley again.

The Young Blogger

At that time, the British Broadcasting Corporation (BBC) approached Malala's father in search of someone who could blog for them about what it was like to live under Taliban rule. It was around this time that Malala adopted the pen name 'Gul Makai' and began writing regular entries for BBC in Urdu about her daily life. She wrote from January through the beginning of March of that year; 35 of those

entries were also translated into English. Meanwhile, the Taliban shut down all girls' schools in Swat and blew up more than 100 of them.

Activism

In February 2009, Malala made her first television appearance, when she was interviewed by Pakistani journalist and talk show host Hamid Mir on the Pakistan current events show Capital Talk.

In early 2009, *The New York Times* reporter Adam Ellick worked with Malala to make a documentary, *Class Dismissed*. It was a 13-minute piece about the school shutdown. Ellick made a second film with her, titled *A Schoolgirl's Odyssey*. *The New York Times* posted both films on their website in 2009. That summer, Malala met with U.S. special envoy to Afghanistan and Pakistan Richard Holbrooke, and asked him to help in her effort to protect the education of girls in Pakistan.

With Malala's continuing television appearances and coverage in the local and international media, it had become apparent by December 2009 that she was the BBC's young blogger. Once her identity was known, she began to receive widespread recognition for her activism.

In October 2011, she was nominated by human rights activist Desmond Tutu for the 'International Children's Peace Prize'. In December the same year she was awarded Pakistan's first 'National Youth Peace Prize' (later renamed the National Malala Peace Prize).

Attempt of Assassination

On October 9, 2012, Malala was shot by a masked gunman who entered her school bus and asked, "Which one of you is Malala? Speak up, otherwise I will shoot at you all."

Malala was identified and she was shot with a single bullet, which went through her head, neck and shoulder. Two other girls were also injured, though not as badly as Malala.

This inhuman attempt on her life received worldwide disapproval and led to protests across Pakistan. Over 2 million people signed the Right to Education campaign. The petition helped the ratification of Pakistan's first Right to Education bill in Pakistan.

Ehsanullah Ehsan, chief spokesman for the Pakistani Taliban, claimed responsibility for the attack on Malala, stating that Malala was a symbol of the infidels and obscenity. However, other Islamic clerics in Pakistan issued a fatwa against the Taliban leaders and said there was no religious justification for shooting a schoolgirl.

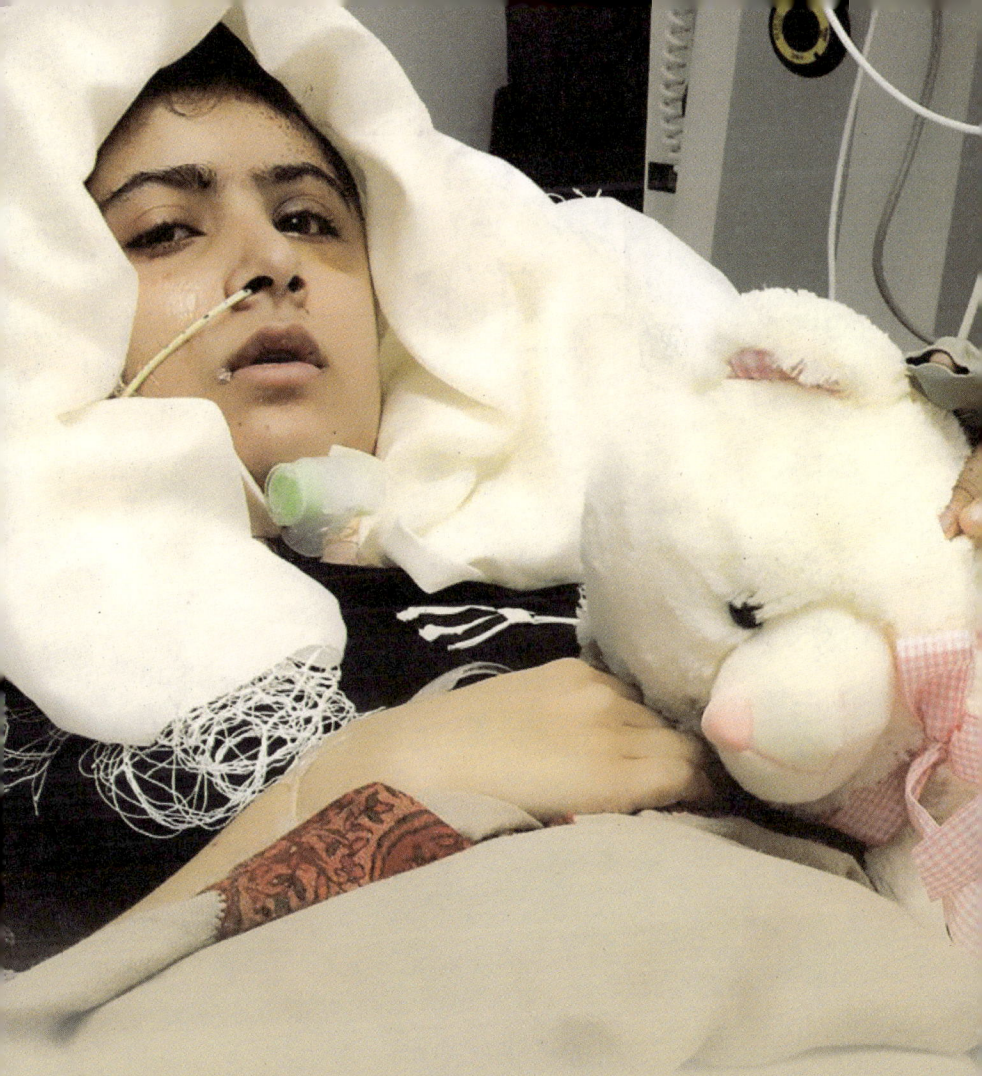

Medical Treatment

After this terrible shooting incident, Malala was airlifted to a military hospital in Peshawar, where doctors were forced to begin operating on her after swelling developed in the left portion of her brain, which had been damaged by the bullet when it passed through her head. After a five-hour-long operation, doctors successfully removed the

bullet, which had lodged in her shoulder near her spinal cord. The doctors at once performed a decompressive craniectomy, in which part of the skull is removed to allow room for the brain to swell.

On October 11, 2012, a panel of Pakistani and British doctors decided to move Malala to the Armed Forces Institute of Cardiology in Rawalpindi. However, it was decided that it would be better if Malala were shifted to Germany, where she could receive the best medical treatment, as soon as she was stable enough to travel. A team of doctors would travel with her, and the government would bear the expenses of her treatment. Doctors reduced Malala's sedation on October 13, and she was able to move all four limbs.

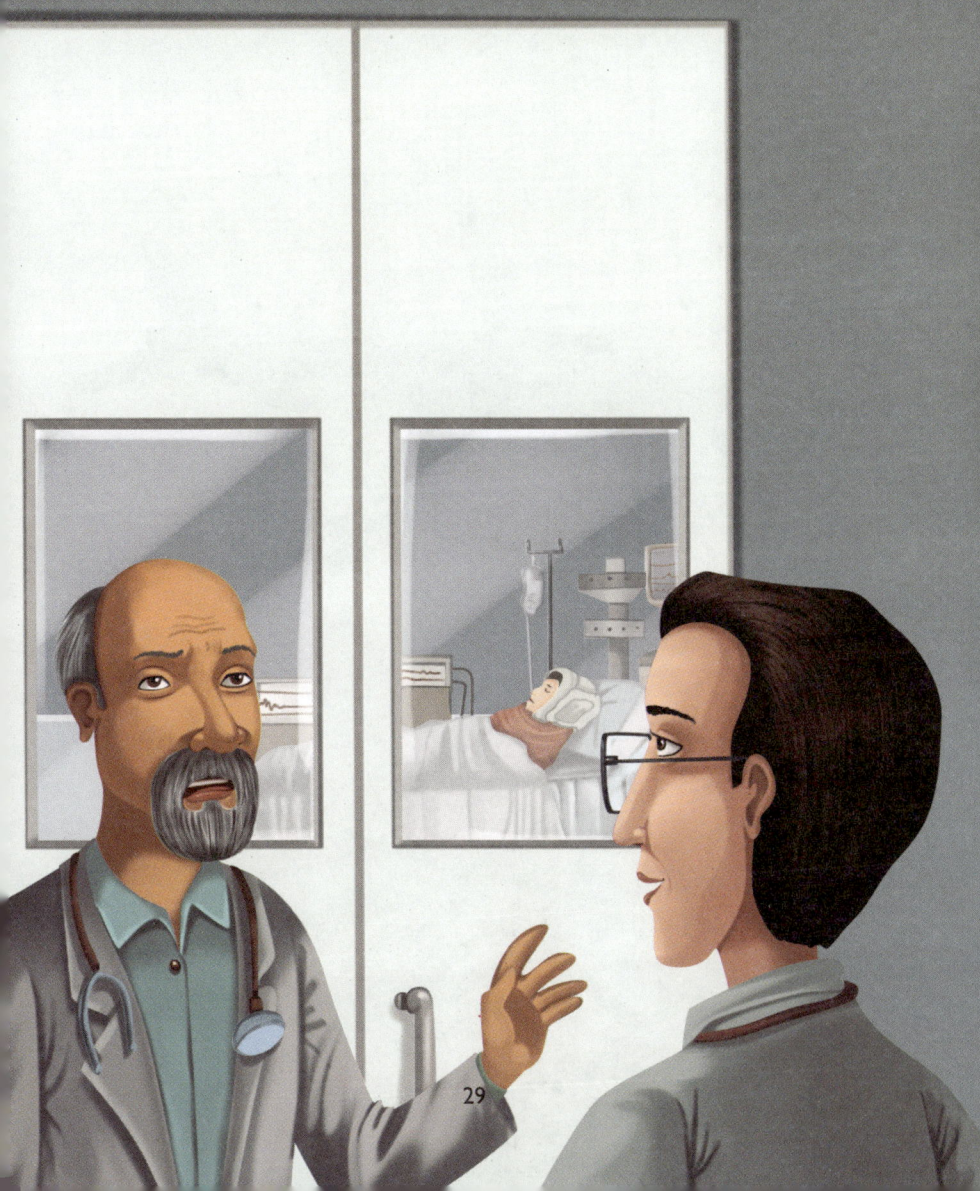

Doctors from all around the world offered their services to cure this 'unique and brave little girl'. On October 15, Malala travelled to the United Kingdom for further treatment, approved by both her doctors and her family. Her plane landed in Abu Dhabi for re-fuelling and then continued to Birmingham, where she was treated at

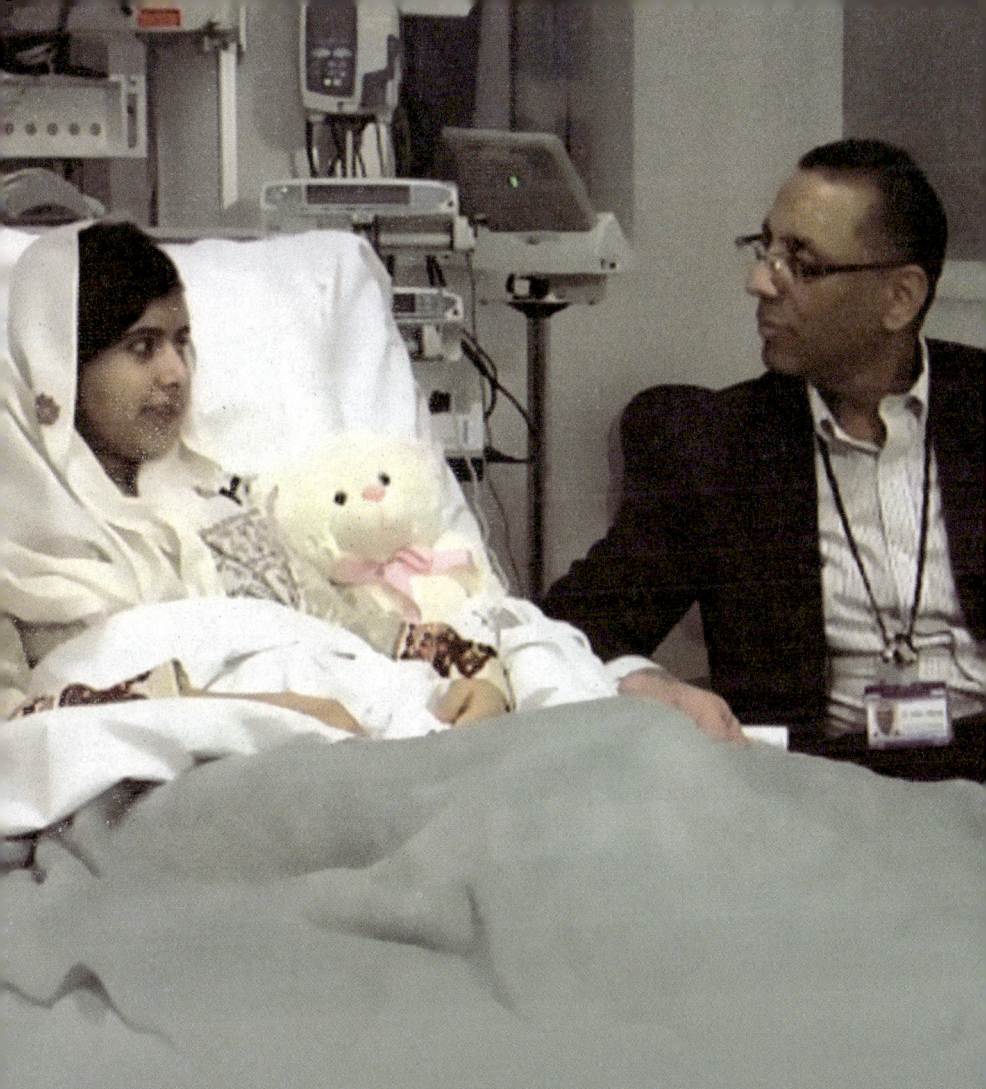

the Queen Elizabeth Hospital. One of the specialties of this hospital was the treatment of military personnel injured in conflict. According to the UK Government, the Pakistani government paid for all transport, medical, accommodation and subsistence costs for Malala and those accompanying her.

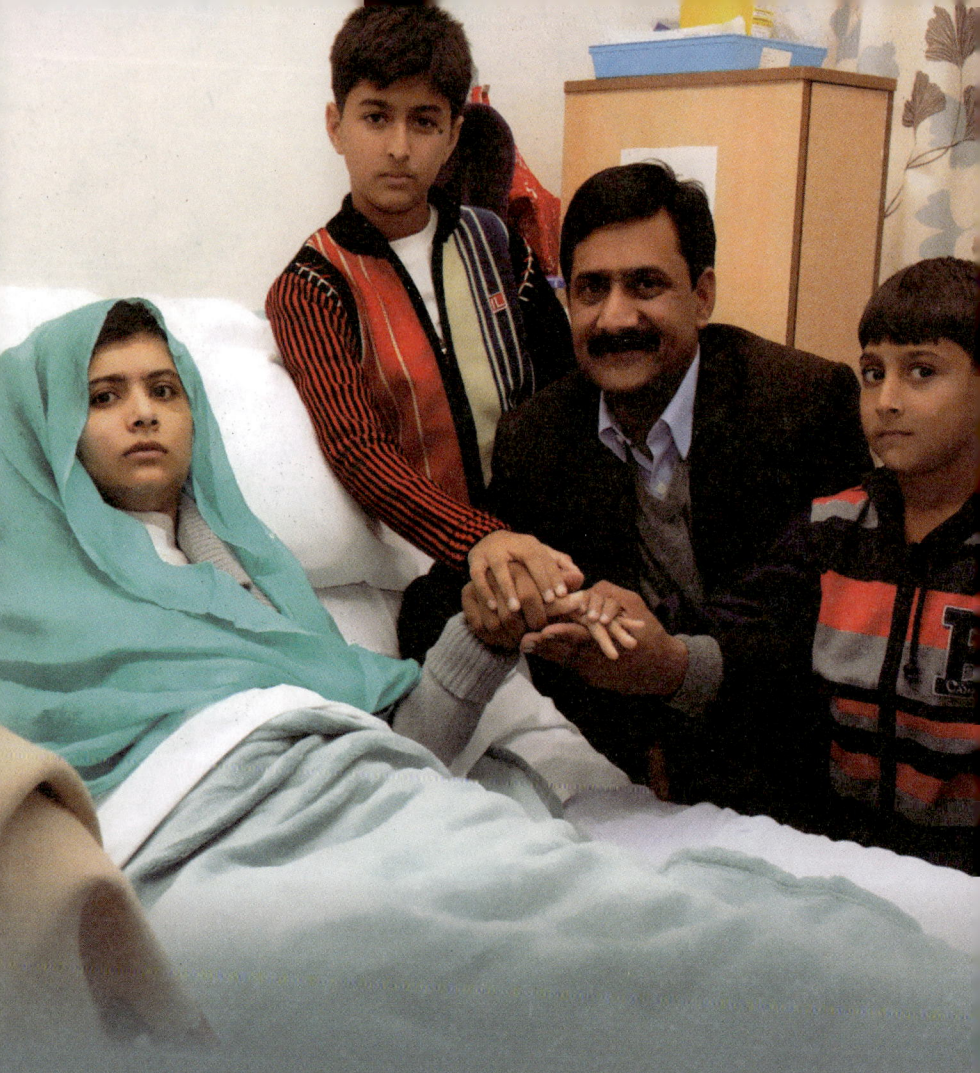

Malala came out of her coma on October 17, 2012. She was responding well to the treatment, and was said to have a good chance of fully recovering without any brain damage. Later updates on October 20 and 21 that year stated that she was stable, but was still battling an infection. By November 8, Malala was photographed sitting up in bed.

On January 3, 2013, Malala was discharged from the Queen Elizabeth Hospital in Birmingham to continue her rehabilitation at her family's temporary home in the West Midlands. She underwent a five-hour long operation on February 2, 2013, to reconstruct her skull and restore her hearing, and was reported to be in a stable condition. She had finally managed to survive the deadly attack.

She joined the all-girls' Edgbaston High School in March 2013, in Birmingham, England.

The assassination attempt on this remarkable girl received worldwide media coverage. It produced a huge wave of sympathy and anger. Protests against the shooting were held in several Pakistani cities the day after the attack.

The Pakistani officials offered Rs. 10 million (US$ 105,000) reward for information leading to the arrest of the attackers. Responding to concerns about his safety, Malala's father said, "We wouldn't leave our country if my daughter survives or not. We have an ideology that advocates peace. The Taliban cannot stop all independent voices through the force of bullets."

The Pakistani President Asif Ali Zardari described the shooting as an attack on 'civilized people'. UN Secretary-General Ban Ki-moon called it a 'heinous and cowardly act'. U.S. President Barack Obama termed the attack 'reprehensible, disgusting and tragic'. He along with his wife Michelle Obama, and their daughter Malia met Malala in the Oval Office on October 11, 2013.

The Secretary of State Hillary Clinton said Malala had been 'very brave in standing up for the rights of girls and that the attackers had been 'threatened by that kind of empowerment'. British Foreign Secretary William Hague called the shooting 'barbaric' and that it had 'shocked Pakistan and the world'.

American singer Madonna dedicated her song 'Human Nature' to Malala at a concert in Los Angeles on the day of the attack. American actress Angelina Jolie wrote an article explaining the event to her children and answering questions like 'Why did those men think they needed to kill Malala?' Jolie later donated US$ 200,000 to the Malala

Fund for girls' education. The former First Lady of the United States Laura Bush wrote a piece in *The Washington Post* in which she compared Malala to Holocaust diarist Anne Frank. Indian director Amjad Khan announced that he would be making a biographical film based on Malala Yousafzai.

In the days that followed the attack, the Taliban tried to justify their terrible act by saying that Malala had been brainwashed by her father.

"We warned him several times to stop his daughter from using dirty language against us, but he did not listen and forced us to take this extreme step."

The Taliban also justified the attack saying that the Quran says 'people propagating against Islam and Islamic forces should be killed.'

After a prolonged investigation, the police arrested six men for involvement in the attack, but they were later released for lack of evidence.

Malala's Protest Continues

Malala spoke before the United Nations in July 2013, and met Queen Elizabeth II in Buckingham Palace. The following September she spoke at Harvard University, and in October she met U.S. President Barack Obama and his family (as mentioned earlier).

In December, she addressed the Oxford Union. The following year, in July, Malala spoke at the Girl Summit in London, advocating for rights for girls. In October the same year, after receiving the World Children's Prize for the rights of the child in Mariefred, Sweden, she announced a donation of US$ 50,000 through the UNRWA, to help rebuild 65 schools in Gaza.

United Nations Petition

On October 15, UN Special Envoy for global education, Gordon Brown, visited Malala and launched a petition in her name. At that time she was in the hospital for her treatment. The petition was, 'In support for what Malala fought for.'

Using the slogan 'I am Malala,' the petition contains three demands:

- We call on Pakistan to agree to a plan to deliver education for every child.
- We call on all countries to outlaw discrimination against girls.
- We call on international organizations to ensure that the world's 61 million out-of-school children are in education by the end of 2015.

Malala's Speech at the United Nations

Malala Day

On July 12, 2013, on Malala's 16th birthday, she spoke at the UN to call for worldwide access to education. The UN named the event as 'Malala Day'. It was her first public speech since the attack, leading the first ever Youth Takeover of the UN, with an audience of over 500 young education advocates from around the world.

Malala's Speech

Malala delivered the following speech at the UN meet:

Honourable UN Secretary General Ban Ki-moon, respected president of the General Assembly Vuk Jeremic, honourable UN envoy for global education Gordon Brown, respected elders and my dear brothers and sisters: Assalamu alaikum.

Today it is an honour for me to be speaking again after a long time. Being here with such honourable people is a great moment in my life and it is an honour for me that today I am wearing a shawl of the late Benazir Bhutto. I don't know where to begin my speech. I don't know what people would be expecting me to say, but first of all thank you to God for whom we all are equal and thank you to every person who has prayed for my fast recovery and new life. I cannot believe how much love people have shown me. I have received thousands of good-wish cards and gifts from all over the world. Thank you to all of them. Thank you to the children whose innocent words encouraged me. Thank you to my elders whose prayers strengthened me. I would like to thank my nurses, doctors and the staff of the hospitals in Pakistan and the UK and the UAE government who have helped me to get better and recover my strength.

I fully support UN Secretary General Ban Ki-moon in his Global Education First Initiative and the work of UN Special Envoy for Global Education Gordon Brown and the respectful president of the UN General Assembly Vuk Jeremic. I thank them for the leadership they continue to give. They continue to inspire all of us to action. Dear brothers and sisters, do remember one thing: Malala Day is not my day. Today is the day of every woman, every boy and every girl who have raised their voice for their rights.

There are hundreds of human rights activists and social workers who are not only speaking for their rights, but who are struggling to achieve their goal of peace, education and equality. Thousands of people have been killed by the terrorists and millions have been injured. I am just one of them. So here I stand, one girl among many. I speak not just for myself, but so those without a voice can be heard. Those who have fought for their rights. Their right to live in peace. Their right to be treated with dignity. Their right to equality of opportunity. Their right to be educated.

Dear friends, on 9 October 2012, the Taliban shot me on the left side of my forehead. They shot my friends, too. They thought that the bullets would silence us, but they failed. And out of that silence came thousands of voices. The terrorists thought they would change my aims and stop my ambitions. But nothing changed in my life except this: weakness, fear and hopelessness died. Strength, power and courage was born. I am the same Malala. My ambitions are the same. My hopes are the same. And my dreams are the same. Dear sisters and brothers, I am not against anyone. Neither am I here to speak in terms of personal revenge against the Taliban or any other terrorist group. I am here to speak for the right of education for every child. I want education for the sons and daughters of the Taliban and all the terrorists and extremists. I do not even hate the Talib who shot me.

Even if there was a gun in my hand and he was standing in front of me, I would not shoot him. This is the compassion I have learned from Mohamed, the prophet of mercy, Jesus Christ and Lord Buddha. This legacy of change I have inherited from Martin Luther King, Nelson Mandela and Mohammed Ali Jinnah.

This is the philosophy of nonviolence that I have learned from Gandhi, Bacha Khan and Mother Teresa. And this is the forgiveness that I have learned from my father and from my mother. This is what my soul is telling me: be peaceful and love everyone.

Dear sisters and brothers, we realise the importance of light when we see darkness. We realise the importance of our voice when we are silenced. In the same way, when we were in Swat, the north of Pakistan, we realised the importance of pens and books when we saw the guns. The wise saying, "The pen is mightier than the sword." It is true. The extremists are afraid of books and pens. The power of education frightens them. They are afraid of women. The power of the voice of women frightens them. This is why they killed 14 innocent students in the recent attack in Quetta. And that is why they kill female teachers. That is why they are blasting schools every day because they are afraid of change and equality that we will bring to our society. And I remember that there was a boy in our school who was asked by a journalist: "Why are the Taliban against education?" He answered very simply by pointing to his book, he said: "A Talib doesn't know what is written inside this book."

They think that God is a tiny, little conservative being who would point guns at people's heads just for going to school. These terrorists are misusing the name of Islam for their own personal benefit. Pakistan is a peace-loving, democratic country. Pashtuns want education for their daughters and sons. Islam is a religion of peace, humanity and brotherhood. It is the duty and responsibility to get education for each child that is what it says. Peace is a necessity for education. In many parts of the world, especially Pakistan and Afghanistan, terrorism, war and conflicts stop children from going to schools. We are really

tired of these wars. Women and children are suffering in many ways in many parts of the world.

In India, innocent and poor children are victims of child labour. Many schools have been destroyed in Nigeria. People in Afghanistan have been affected by extremism. Young girls have to do domestic child labour and are forced to get married at an early age. Poverty, ignorance, injustice, racism and the deprivation of basic rights are the main problems, faced by both men and women.

Today, I am focusing on women's rights and girls' education because they are suffering the most. There was a time when women activists asked men to stand up for their rights. But this time we will do it by ourselves. I am not telling men to step away from speaking for women's rights, but I am focusing on women to be independent and fight for themselves. So dear sisters and brothers, now it's time to speak up. So today, we call upon the world leaders to change their strategic policies in favour of peace and prosperity. We call upon the world leaders that all of these deals must protect women and children's rights. A deal that goes against the rights of women is unacceptable.

We call upon all governments to ensure free, compulsory education all over the world for every child. We call upon all the governments to fight against terrorism and violence. To protect children from brutality and harm. We call upon the developed nations to support the expansion of education opportunities for girls in the developing world.

We call upon all communities to be tolerant, to reject prejudice based on caste, creed, sect, colour, religion or agenda, to ensure freedom and equality for women so they can flourish. We cannot all succeed when half of us are held back. We call upon our sisters around the world to be brave, to embrace the strength within themselves and realise their full potential.

Dear brothers and sisters, we want schools and education for every child's bright future. We will continue our

journey to our destination of peace and education. No one can stop us. We will speak up for our rights and we will bring change to our voice. We believe in the power and the strength of our words. Our words can change the whole world because we are all together, united for the cause of education. And if we want to achieve our goal, then let us empower ourselves with the weapon of knowledge and let us shield ourselves with unity and togetherness.

Dear brothers and sisters, we must not forget that millions of people are suffering from poverty and injustice and ignorance. We must not forget that millions of children are out of their schools. We must not forget that our sisters and brothers are waiting for a bright, peaceful future.

So let us wage a glorious struggle against illiteracy, poverty and terrorism, let us pick up our books and our pens, they are the most powerful weapons. One child, one teacher, one book and one pen can change the world. Education is the only solution. Education first. Thank you.

Knowing Malala

It stands to no doubt after so many things happening to Malala that she is intelligent and more ambitious, as compared to other girls in the society that she lives in. She says, "It's hard for girls in our society to be anything other than teachers or doctors, if they can work at all. I was different—I never hid my desire when I changed from wanting to be a doctor to wanting to be an inventor or a politician."

Malala is definitely not a person to bow down and accept things imposed on her. She has a rebellious nature and chooses to rebel against the traditions that suppress women.

"I knew as we got older, the girls would be expected to stay inside. We'd be expected to cook and serve our brothers and fathers…this was the tradition. I had decided very early I would not be like that."

"I am proud to be a Pashtun, but…our code of conduct has a lot to answer for, particularly where the treatment of women is concerned."

Again, it is worth noting that Malala is very wise for her age and is quick to learn from her mistakes.

"I think everyone makes a mistake at least once in their life. The important thing is what you learn from it."

She idolizes Mahatma Gandhi and Khan Abdul Ghaffar Khan, and believes in the non-violent philosophy advocated by them.

Malala is a compassionate person and cares for the less fortunate. She keeps persuading her father to provide 'free places' at the school to the scavenger children of the rubbish mountain. Many families did not want to pay school fees for their girls. To enable these girls to study, Malala would coax her father to offer free seats.

Malala has a keen sense of justice and wants to change the world for the better. She often appeals to God: "God, give me strength and courage and make me perfect because I want to make this world perfect."

Courageous

Ambitious

Compassionate

Leader

She sees the injustice committed by militants and is infuriated by their misinterpretation of religion. She resents the Taliban and their attempt to enforce their code of conduct on the people.

"We felt like the Taliban saw us as little dolls to control, telling us what to do and how to dress," she once stated.

Courage is another very important trait that Malala displays. She has always shown immense courage by speaking out against the Taliban in support of girls' right to education.

"In my heart was the belief that God would protect me. If I am speaking for my rights, for the rights of girls, I am not doing anything wrong," she said.

She had once challenged the Taliban saying, "How dare the Taliban take away my basic right to education?"

Malala has many leadership qualities as well and she uses them to change the views of people around her. She realizes the power of words when she starts giving interviews and writing diary entries for the BBC website about life under the Taliban.

She once said, "I began to see that the pen and the words that come from it can be much more powerful than machine guns, tanks or helicopters ... we were learning how powerful we are when we speak."

She also recognizes her abilities and has decided to become a politician.

"I had thought about becoming a politician and now I know that was the right choice. Our country had so many crises and no real leaders to tackle them," she stated.

Malala has received many awards for supporting girls' right to education, but she remains as humble as the little girl that she was back in the Swat Valley. She believes, "I knew that any of the girls in my class could have achieved what I had achieved if they had had their parents' support."

She viewed the awards and recognition as if "they were little jewels without much meaning." Malala has shown immense will power as she fought to survive the horrific injury inflicted by the gunshot. She bore her pain with fortitude and is determined to continue her campaign for girls' right to education. "It feels like this life is a second life. People prayed to God to spare me, and I was spared for a reason—to use my life for helping people," she maintained.

Awards and Accolades

Among her many awards, Malala won the United Nations Human Rights Prize in 2013, which is awarded every five years. She was named one of *Time* magazine's most influential people in 2013, and she appeared on one of the seven covers that were printed for that issue. With Christina Lamb (foreign correspondent for *The Sunday Times*), Malala co-authored a memoir, *I Am Malala: The Girl Who Stood Up for Education and Was Shot by the Taliban* (2013).

In 2014, Malala became the youngest person to win the Liberty Medal, awarded by the National Constitution

Centre in Philadelphia to public figures striving for people's freedom throughout the world. Nominated for the Nobel Peace Prize in 2013, Malala became the youngest recipient of the award in 2014.

Malala is respected the world over and will always be remembered as a fearless girl who fought for education and who fought for children's rights even in the face of death.

Timeline

- **1997** Malala is born on July 12, in Mingora, Pakistan

- **2008** The Taliban begin to target girls' schools and force them to close down

  Malala's father's school remains open, but is under constant threat

  Malala, at 11 years of age, gives a speech in front of national press titled, "How Dare the Taliban Take Away My Basic Right to an Education"

- **2009** The Taliban orders all girls' schools to close

  Malala begins blogging for the British Broadcasting Company (BBC) Urdu site using a pseudonym

- **2009** Pakistani army launches an attack in Swat Valley; Malala and her family evacuate

- **2009** Taliban is pushed out of Swat and Malala's family returns home

- **2010** Threatening notes begin to appear under Malala's door ordering her to end the crusade

Timeline

- **2011** The President of Pakistan awards Malala with the first ever National Youth Peace Prize

- **2012** Malala is shot by the Taliban while travelling home from school

    The UNSEGE start a petition allowing girls to go to school; over a million people sign the petition

- **2012** Malala is the 'runner-up' for Time magazine's 'Person of the Year'

- **2013** Malala gave a speech at the United Nations; it was also her birthday; the day is recognized as 'Malala Day'

- **2013** Malala is nominated for the Nobel Peace Prize

- **2013** Malala recovers in Birmingham, U.K. and starts attending high school

- **2013** Malala's memoir 'I Am Malala' is released

- **2014** Men involved in shooting Malala are arrested

- **2014** Malala wins Nobel Peace Prize

Project Work

What is your idea of the country Pakistan? Form groups of four and make a project on this country. Focus on the following points:
- Geographical location of Pakistan
- People
- Languages spoken
- Popular food
- Tourist spots

Class Discussion

As future citizens of this world, what according to you are the global problems today. Discuss the issues in class with your teacher and classmates. Do not forget to focus on the solutions to these problems also.

Pair and Share

Write down a few sentences about 10 people globally who have brought a difference in the world of ours. They can be from any field—education, politics, art, literature, etc.

Share your notes with your partner. Do read what your partner has written.

Questions

1. Who is Malala?
2. What does her name mean?
3. Where did she live originally?
4. Why is she considered remarkable?
5. When did she get Nobel Prize and for what?
6. Name Malala's father.
7. Name the other members of her family.
8. Which school in Pakistan did she go to?
9. What was her pen name when she blogged for BBC?
10. Why was Malala shot by Taliban militants?
11. Where was Malala treated?
12. Where did she relocate to after she recovered? Name the school she attended there.
13. What was the global reaction after Malala was shot?
14. Describe Malala's character briefly.
15. Enumerate some of the awards that she was honoured with.

Glossary

accommodation: a room or a building in which someone may live

activism: the action of using vigorous campaigning to bring about political or social changes

administered: be responsible for the running of a business or organization

ambitious: having a strong desire to succeed

artillery: a military branch of the armed forces that uses large-calibre guns

assassination: the murder of someone important for political or religious reasons

barbaric: savagely cruel

blog: a regularly updated website or web page, run by an individual or small group, that is written in an informal style

campaign: a series of military operations intended to achieve a goal

co-author: to jointly author something

compassionate: feeling sympathy and concern for others

courageous: brave, fearless

cowardly: lacking courage

Glossary

criticism: the expression of disapproval of someone or something

damage: physical harm of something

disapproval: unfavourable opinion about something or someone

edict: an official proclamation issued by a person in authority

emulate: to imitate someone

established: having existed or done something for a long time

ethics: moral principles that govern a person's behaviour

expenditures: to spend funds

exploitation: treating someone unfairly in order to benefit from their work

ferocious: cruel or violent

gender: the state of being male or female

heinous: utterly wicked

horrific: something that causes horror

humanitarian: seeking to promote human welfare

Glossary

identified: to indicate who or what someone or something is

incident: an event

infection: the process of infecting

infuriated: to make someone extremely angry

injury: a hurt

injustice: lack of fairness

investigation: finding about something

justice: the quality of being reasonable

leadership: the action of leading a group of people

memoir: a historical description or biography written from personal knowledge

migration: movement of animals from one region to another on the basis of seasons

militants: a group of people who use violent methods in support of a political or social cause

misinterpretation: the act of interpreting something wrongly

Pashun: any Pashto-speaking person of Afghanistan or Pakistan

politician: a person who is professionally involved in politics

Glossary

prohibition: to forbid something by law

rebellious: showing a desire to resist authority

selfless: concerned more with the needs of others than with one's own

submissive: meekly obedient

Taliban: an Islamic fundamentalist political movement in Afghanistan

terrible: extremely bad or serious

translate: to express the sense of words in another language

violence: to apply physical force to hurt, damage, or kill someone